Published in the United States by Random House Children's Books, a division of Penguin Random House LLC, 1745 Broadway, New York, NY 10019, and in Canada by Penguin Random House Canada Limited, Toronto, in conjunction with Sesame Workshop. Originally published in a different form by Western Publishing Company, Inc., Racine, WI, in 1976.

Random House and the colophon are registered trademarks of Penguin Random House LLC.

Visit us on the Web!
rhcbooks.com
SesameStreetBooks.com
www.sesamestreet.org

Educators and librarians, for a variety of teaching tools, visit us at RHTeachersLibrarians.com

ISBN 978-1-9848-9432-8 (trade) — ISBN 978-1-9848-9433-5 (ebook)

MANUFACTURED IN CHINA 10 9 8 7 6 5 4 3 2 1

Random House Children's Books supports the First Amendment and celebrates the right to read.

HOW TO BE A GROUCH

Written and Illustrated by Caroll E. Spinney
(Alias: Oscar the Grouch)

Random House New York

BY THE
GREATEST
GROUCH
IN THE
WORLD!

FIRST OF ALL-
IF YOU WANT TO BE A GROUCH,
YOU'LL HAVE TO STOP BEING SO
NICE AND CUTE!

NEXT- LEARN TO FROWN!

WHAT GROUCHES LOOK LIKE
GROUCHY ME
CITY GROUCH
COUNTRY GROUCH
GROUCHY STOREKEEPER
ANGER CEREAL
GROUCHY PERSON
GROUCHY DOG
NASTY
GROUCHY CAT

WHERE GROUCHES LIVE
IN TRASH CANS
(MY FAVORITE)
SCRAM
SOMETIMES
IN OLD CARS
GO AWAY!
IN CRUMMY OLD HOUSES
HIT THE ROAD!
OR EVEN
IN YUCCHY BEAUTIFUL HOUSES!

WHAT GROUCHES EAT
A PICKLE SPLIT
CHUNKY
FISH ICE CREAM
HOT BEEF STEW WITH
CHOCOLATE GRAVY IN A MELON!
HOT DOG WITH
SPAGHETTI AND ORANGES!

HOW TO BAKE A GROUCH PIE
FIRST, ROLL THE DOUGH!
PUT THE DOUGH IN A PIE PAN.
(I USE AN OLD HUBCAP!)
FILL IT WITH
THINGS YOU HATE TO EAT!
DON'T
COOK IT.
SERVE IT TO YOUR FRIENDS.
WHAT FRIENDS?

HOW GROUCHES TRAVEL
OSCAR'S
TRASH CAN SPECIAL
THIS IS THE
FAMILY MODEL!
WORLD'S FASTEST
TRASH CAN CYCLE!
TRASH CAN SPORTS CAR

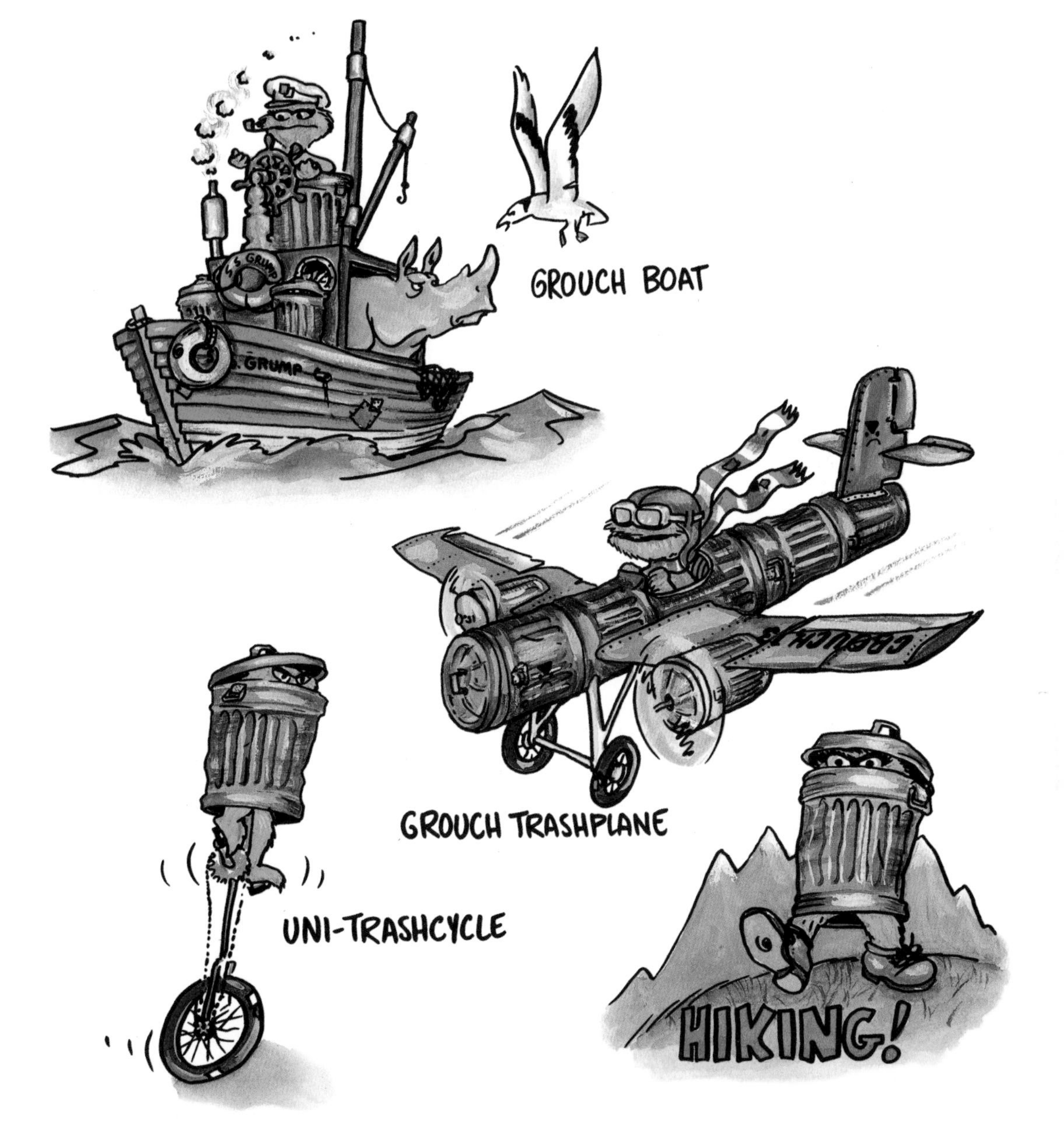
GROUCH BOAT
S.S. GRUMP
S.S. GRUMP
GROUCH TRASHPLANE
UNI-TRASHCYCLE
HIKING!

IF YOU WANT TO BE A GROUCH, IT HELPS TO BE TIRED AND GRUMPY, SO—
GET A BAD NIGHT'S SLEEP!
OSCAR
FIRST, PUT ROCKS UNDER YOUR SHEET.
OSCAR
THEN, SLEEP WITH YOUR HEAD ON THE FLOOR.
YOU WILL WAKE UP GROUCHY!

AND BY THE WAY, BEFORE YOU GO TO SLEEP,
EAT FRIED CHICKEN WITH ICE CREAM AND PEA SOUP ON IT.
YOU WILL HAVE GROUCHY DREAMS!
RR
Uncle Billy

GETTING THE DAY OFF TO A GROUCHY START
SET YOUR ALARM CLOCK TO GO OFF TOO EARLY!
MAKE SURE IT'S LOUD!
THUNK.
OSCAR
BE SURE TO GET UP ON THE WRONG SIDE OF THE BED!
TELL YOURSELF HOW GROUCHY YOU LOOK THIS MORNING.
COLD TURKEY GRAVY ON YOUR CORNFLAKES WILL ALWAYS MAKE YOU...
VERY, VERY GROUCHY!

THINGS THAT HELP MAKE ME GROUCHY
BIRDS THAT SING!
BIRTHDAYS MAKE ME GROUCHY!
GO AWAY!
OSCAR
SOMEBODY SAYING HELLO MAKES ME GROUCHY!
U.S. MAIL
NOBODY SAYING HELLO MAKES ME GROUCHY!

MORE GROUCHY THINGS
THE BUBBLE GUM MACHINE THAT TAKES MY MONEY BUT DOESN'T GIVE ME ANYTHING!
MY BEACH CHAIR IS OFTEN VERY GROUCHY!
EVEN I HATE IT WHEN HORNETS ARE GROUCHY!

GRRR!
A DOG GNAWING ON A BONE IS GROUCHY-IF YOU **BOTHER** HIM!
HEE HEE HAW!
WHACK!
SOMEONE WHO THINKS HE'S FUNNY, BUT ISN'T, MAKES ME VERY GROUCHY!
COAT HANGERS CAN BE THE WORLD'S GROUCHIEST THINGS!

HOW DO GROUCHES RELAX?
I LIKE TO PLAY MY BROKEN RECORDS.
LET A FROWN BE YOUR UMBRELLA
WHAT A ROTTEN DAY!
MY TV SET IS BROKEN, SO I WATCH MY PET WORM, SLIMEY.
HIS SHOW IS REALLY CRUMMY!

GOING TO A GROUCH MOVIE
LAST WEEK
THE GROUCH THAT ATE RACINE
COMING
THE GROUCH THAT ROARED
TICKETS
TODAY
HOW GREEN WAS MY GROUCH
STARRING Ingrid GROUCH
FIRST, YOU WAIT IN A VERY SLOW TICKET LINE.
THEN A GROUCHY USHER YELLS AT YOU TO GET YOUR FEET OFF THE SEAT.
THE BEST PART COMES WHEN THE MOVIE MACHINE BREAKS DOWN!

HOW TO TAKE A GROUCH VACATION
EXPRESS
SEATS 36
BUS STOP
GET ON THE GROUCH EXPRESS BUS.
IT'S ALWAYS THREE HOURS LATE.
RIDE NINE HOURS WITHOUT STOPPING FOR LUNCH!
MUDVILLE FLATS INN
GO AWAY
YOU ARE NOT WELCOME
VACANCY
AT LAST! MUDVILLE FLATS INN IS WHERE WISE GROUCHES STAY!

VACATION FUN
WATCH THE RAINDROPS RUN DOWN THE WINDOWS. IT ALMOST ALWAYS RAINS IN MUDVILLE FLATS.
GO FOR A STROLL IN THE FAMOUS GARDENS.
TAKE THE GRAND TOUR OF THE MUDVILLE FLATS DUMP!

GROUCHES LIKE TO BE WITH OTHER GROUCHES, SO WHY NOT JOIN A GROUCH CLUB? I BELONG TO THE
DISAGREEABLE ORDER OF GROUCHES (D.O.G.).
ME
D.O.G.
D.O.G.
D.O.G.
D.O.G.
D.O.G.
D.O.G.
D.O.G.
D.O.G.
PIG
Bad Luck!
THIS PICTURE WAS TAKEN LAST YEAR. I AM NOW PAST PRESIDENT OF D.O.G., AND I AM GROUCHIER THAN EVER!

MY GROUCH FAMILY
MOM
POP
GRAM
MY BABY BROTHER, OTTO. HE'S ONLY ONE, AND HE'S A GROUCH ALREADY!
THIS IS MY COUSIN, SMILING GEORGE. OH, WELL, WE CAN'T ALL BE PERFECT!

STORYBOOK GROUCHES
HERE ARE SOME GROUCHES YOU MIGHT KNOW.
THE GIANT AT THE TOP OF JACK'S BEANSTALK
CINDERELLA'S FAMILY
WITCHES ARE ALMOST ALWAYS GROUCHY!

MOST STORYBOOK DRAGONS ARE VERY GROUCHY!
PRESENTING
THE
GREATEST
GROUCH
IN THE
WORLD!
ME!

AND THE WINNER THIS YEAR IS CATHY CROTCHET OF PODUNK, MASS. SHE WINS THE GROUCH AWARD AND A ONE-WAY TICKET TO MUDVILLE FLATS. (NOW SHE'S **REALLY** GROUCHY!)

IF YOU FOLLOW THE ADVICE IN **THIS BOOK**, MAYBE YOU'LL WIN NEXT YEAR!

REMEMBER THESE THINGS THAT A GROUCH CAN'T STAND
FRIENDLY PUPPY DOGS
PRETTY FLOWERS
CUDDLY KITTENS
MUSHY MAIL!
BE MY VALENTINE
XXX Maria

LEARN TO BE MISERABLE

GETTING NEW TRASH MAKES ME HAPPY, BUT I DON'T LIKE BEING HAPPY!

BEING HAPPY MAKES ME MISERABLE, AND I LOVE BEING MISERABLE!

SO THAT MAKES ME HAPPY – WHICH MAKES ME MISERABLE!

HAVE GROUCHY DAYS
I LOVE THE RAIN!
I LOVE THE WIND!
I LOVE ICY SNOW!
BUT... I HATE THE WARM, FRIENDLY SUN!
NOW TURN THE PAGE FOR MY BEST ADVICE!

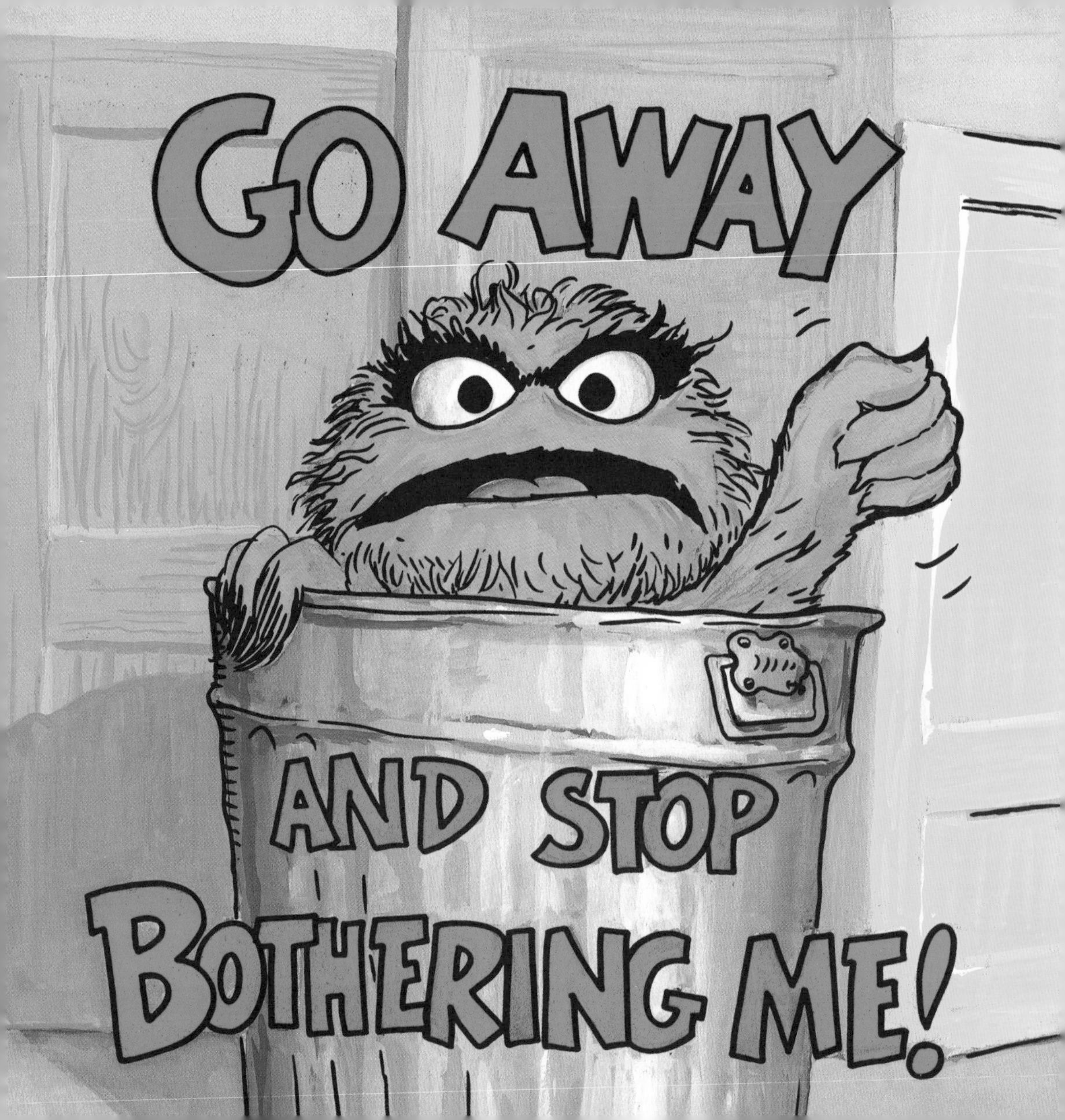
GO AWAY
AND STOP
BOTHERING ME!

CTW
SESAME STREET
Abby's
SPINNEY

MEET CAROLL SPINNEY

Caroll Spinney performed Oscar the Grouch on Sesame Street for more than four decades, sharing the legendary—and very dirty—trash can with Oscar. In fact, he understands grouches so well, Oscar chose him personally to write and illustrate this guide to being a grouch.

During those years on Sesame Street, Caroll also performed as Big Bird, the curious, sweet-tempered, eight-foot-two-inch yellow avian beloved by fans the world over.

A born-and-bred New Englander (if you listen carefully, you can hear a little bit of Yankee twang in Big Bird's and Oscar's voices), Caroll is also a fine artist. His black-and-white sketches and watercolor portraits of his many Sesame Street friends are represented by Arts & Framing of Putnam, a gallery in Connecticut.